This book belongs to:

For my sisters

L.M.G.

For Edward

R.S.

First published in 2008 by Meadowside Children's Books
185 Fleet Street London EC4A 2HS
www.meadowsidebooks.com

Illustrations © Rachel Swirles
The right of Rachel Swirles to be identified as the illustrator
of this work has been asserted by her in accordance with
the Copyright, Designs and Patents Act, 1988

A CIP catalogue record for this book
is available from the British Library
10 9 8 7 6 5 4 3 2 1
Printed in Indonesia

The Snow Queen

Retold by Lucy M George and illustrated by Rachel Swirles

meadowside
CHILDREN'S BOOKS

n a little town, not so far from here,
lived a boy and a girl. They were best
friends and their names were Kay and Gerda.

Kay and Gerda lived next door to one another.
From their windows they would play games,
pass secret notes, and talk all day,
(and sometimes whisper all night).

Everywhere they went, they went together. Everything they did, they did together. And every secret they had, they told each other. Every single one.

To my best friend xx

Kay loved the spring and Gerda loved the autumn,

but both of them loved the winter.

At the first sight of snow, they would drag Kay's
wonky old sledge to the hill and then ride it
all the way to the frozen lake, falling off
into the soft snow and laughing
as they went.

When it was cold enough
the lake froze so thick
that the children could
skate upon it.

ne day, some of the older children started talking about an evil queen. A queen who lived in the frozen hills. A queen who lived in a palace of ice.

The Snow Queen.

"She comes down here to steal children," said the oldest boy. "She blows enchanted snow into your face, then you have to go with her," he said.

"My grandmother told me she steals you from your bed and you can never come back because she makes you so cold, you forget who you are and where you live," said another one.

Kay was scared of the stories about the
Snow Queen and he told Gerda
on the way home.

"Nothing could ever make me forget you!"
promised Gerda. "Even if your heart
was frozen, and no one remembered you,
and you didn't even know who you were!
Even then.

I would remember you. I promise!"

And so they carried on up the hill,
throwing snow, laughing and dreaming
of the hot chocolate that awaited
them at home, all thoughts of
the Snow Queen gone.

ne night, Gerda had a terrible nightmare. She was lost in the forest, shouting for Kay, but he was so fur away, he seemed to be in another world. There was a reindeer trying to help her, but just as she was about to touch it, she awoke with a start.

She hurried into her winter
clothes and went outside
to meet Kay.

But he wasn't there.
No one was.

Instead, there was only a set
of wonky sledge tracks.
Kay's sledge tracks. And instead
of leading down to the lake,
they were leading up into the
frozen mountains.

Gerda rushed to Kay's
door, but when his mother
answered it she didn't know
a boy called Kay.

No one knew
a boy called Kay.

She pictured Kay alone
and afraid. She knew what
she had to do.

erda didn't think about how far she would have to go. She just followed the tracks, all the time thinking of her friend and how afraid he must be.

She walked for many hours and snow began to fall, covering the tracks that Kay's sledge had left.

The harder she tried to
picture Kay's laughing
face, the harder the snow
fell and the harder it
became to follow his tracks,
until eventually, the snow
completely covered them.

She stood in the midst of a
thicket of bracken and nettles
and could only guess which
way to go now.

ust as she felt all hope drain from her, something light seemed to move in the darkness.

A reindeer! It was warm and seemed so kind and gentle. Gerda was sure it was the reindeer from her dream. It was trying to help her.

She climbed onto its back
and it leapt forwards, carrying her
easily over the uneven frozen ground.
They pushed further and further into the frozen
mountains and just when Gerda thought that they
couldn't get any higher, they turned a corner.

An enormous palace of ice came into view.

Gerda could only gasp. It was the Snow Queen's
palace. It was true. She took a deep breath
and thought of Kay.

How afraid he must be!

Then she set off alone
across the frozen wasteland,
turning only to wave fondly
at the reindeer.

 ooner than she wished, Gerda was walking through the cold corridors of the Snow Queen's palace, silently padding over the frozen floor, desperately seeking Kay.

Strange noises echoed around the empty halls.

Then, she saw something.

It was Kay.
He was sitting on the cold floor,
staring into thin air.

"Kay, it's me!" she cried.

But Kay
just stared at her,
confused.

"Kay!" Gerda cried, shaking him,
but he just looked at her blankly.

Gerda was helpless. She pulled
at him, as if to try and drag him,
but he was like a dead weight.

Finally, she fell to the
floor, put her arms around
her friend and sobbed.

But as she cried,
her warm tears fell
onto Kay

and something
happened.

Kay's frozen heart began
to melt, and the Snow
Queen's evil spell was lifted.

Finally he knew who she was.

Kay smiled and laughed at
the sight of his friend.
"You remembered me!"

uddenly the Snow Queen appeared, screaming and trying to snatch Kay back from Gerda.

"No!" she screeched wildly. "You cannot take him! He's mine!"

She was furious, but when she tried
to grab Kay, he was so warm that her
cold hands burned as she touched him!

There was no time to waste!

They sped through
the palace halls...

... and burst out into the fresh air.
The palace of ice had disappeared
and with it, the Snow Queen too.

She had been defeated!
Never again would she
be able to steal children.

And no one ever forgot what Gerda had done for her friend, especially not Kay!